My Dad's a
Balloon

by Malachy Doyle
Illustrated by Peter Utton

W
FRANKLIN WATTS
LONDON•SYDNEY

First published in 2010 by
Franklin Watts
338 Euston Road
London
NW1 3BH

Franklin Watts Australia
Level 17/207 Kent Street
Sydney
NSW 2000

A CIP catalogue record for this book is available
from the British Library.

ISBN 978 0 7496 9428 9 (hbk)
ISBN 978 0 7496 9433 3 (pbk)

Series Editor: Jackie Hamley
Series Advisor: Catherine Glavina
Series Designer: Peter Scoulding

Printed in China

To find out more about Malachy Doyle
and his books, please visit:
www.malachydoyle.com

Franklin Watts is a division of
Hachette Children's Books,
an Hachette UK company
www.hachette.co.uk

My dad's a balloon!

When I blow his little finger,

he gets bigger ...

... and bigger ...

... and **bigger** ...

... till he's a great big bubble
and I'm scared he's going to POP!

"Hold on!" he cries,
and he circles round the room,
all pumped up and bulgy.

Then slowly, slowly, we start to rise,
up off the floor, higher and higher,
till my hair's brushing the ceiling!

9

"Don't let go of my finger!" he yells.

But I have to, I know I have to,

or I'll keep going up till I'm squashed,

flat against the top of the room!

So I let go of his finger.

But as soon as I do,

he's twisting and turning,

faster and faster.

He's zooming all around and going

Wheeeeeeeeeeeeeeeeeeeeeeeeeeeee!

He's spinning and he's whirling,
he's bashing and he's crashing,
off the walls and through the door
and out into the garden.

"Look out, Dad!" I yell.
"You'll fly off into the sky
and I'll never see you again!"

17

I'm chasing behind,
rushing to catch him.
I'm racing behind,
and he's up in a tree.

I'm grabbing his shoe
and it's off in my hand,
and he's up in the air,
once again!

"Stop! Please stop!"
And I'm closing my eyes.
I'm frightened to look
and I'm scared he'll be gone,
up with the clouds, away!

Oh, is it my dad?
Or is it a balloon?
And what am I
going to do?

And then there's a hissing,
from somewhere behind me.
A hushed sort of hissing,
a tired sort of hissing.

It's back on the grass
and it's wibbling, wobbling,
hushing and shushing,
the air nearly gone.

It's smaller and smaller,
slower and slow,
till it slumps to the ground,
exhausted.

I'm standing above it.

I stare in its face.

And it's only **my dad**,

flat on the grass, smiling!

Then I throw myself down
and we're there, side by side.
So there's me and my dad,
flat on the grass, laughing!

"Do it again, Dad!" I yell.

"Do it again!"

Puzzle 1

Put these pictures in the correct order.
Now try writing the story in your own words!

Puzzle 2

Choose the correct speech bubbles for each character. Can you think of any others? Turn over to find the answers.

Answers

Puzzle 1

The correct order is: 1f, 2c, 3e, 4b, 5d, 6a

Puzzle 2

Sam: 1, 3, 6

Dad: 2, 4, 5

Look out for more great Hopscotch stories:

AbracaDebra
ISBN 978 0 7496 9427 2*
ISBN 978 0 7496 9432 6

Bless You!
ISBN 978 0 7496 9429 6*
ISBN 978 0 7496 9434 0

Marigold's Bad Hair Day
ISBN 978 0 7496 9430 2*
ISBN 978 0 7496 9435 7

Mrs Bootle's Boots
ISBN 978 0 7496 9431 9*
ISBN 978 0 7496 9436 4

How to Teach a Dragon Manners
ISBN 978 0 7496 5873 1

The Best Den Ever
ISBN 978 0 7496 5876 2

The Princess and the Frog
ISBN 978 0 7496 5129 9

I Can't Stand It!
ISBN 978 0 7496 5765 9

The Truth about those Billy Goats
ISBN 978 0 7496 5766 6

Izzie's Idea
ISBN 978 0 7496 5334 7

Clever Cat
ISBN 978 0 7496 5131 2

"Sausages!"
ISBN 978 0 7496 4707 0

The Truth about Hansel and Gretel
ISBN 978 0 7496 4708 7

The Queen's Dragon
ISBN 978 0 7496 4618 9

Plip and Plop
ISBN 978 0 7496 4620 2

Find out more about all the Hopscotch books at:
www.franklinwatts.co.uk

*hardback